MW00886851

I would like to dedicate this book to anyone of any age who has ever dealt with a bully. Also to everyone who said I could not accomplish something, thank you for the motivation.

- Kenneth L. Doane II

NOTE TO THE READER:

"I would like to sincerely thank Nichols College for helping bring this dream of mine into fruition, for believing in me, and for the best college education in the world.

I would also like to thank Todd Civin and Civin Media Relations for continually helping me step by step in my pursuit of publishing *Billy's Bully*."

Billy's Bully

Requests for permission to excerpt or make copies of any part of the work should be submitted online at info@mascotbooks.com or mailed to Mascot Books, 560 Herndon Parkway #120, Herndon, VA 20170.

PRT0513A

Library of Congress Control Number: 2013936211

Printed in the United States

ISBN-13: 9781620861349
ISBN-10: 1620861348

www.mascotbooks.com

Billy's Bully

Kenneth L. Doane II

Illustrated by Jay Boucher

Billy, the new kid, is a well-behaved boy.

He plays after school with his newest friend, Joy.

When the school day is over, they laugh and they run,
Play video games, and have so much fun.

Sam lives across town at the end of the street.

His clothes always dirty with black sneakers on his feet.

Sam wears ratty clothing his mom would not choose,

With each game they play, Billy tends to lose.

Sam knocks down Billy; he hits and they fight

All through the day and into the night.

Billy gets angry when Sam tells a lie,

Then Sam stomps his sneakers and makes Billy cry.

Sam beats him soundly in each schoolyard game.

He tells him he's dumb and calls him "so lame."

When Sam gets in trouble, he blames it on Billy.

He calls him a loser and tells him he's silly.

Billy gets angry and thinks of revenge.
He thinks of a plan that will win in the end.
Joy reminds Billy, "That just is not right!
It's a way that is certain to lose at this fight."

But Billy finds Sam to rant and to rave.
He says he'll return soon to show him who's brave.

Sam laughs at Billy, "You're just a dumb fool." Sam knocks down Billy and says, "You're not cool."

Sam's uncalled actions make Joy feel so sad.

He calls her bad names which makes Billy mad.

Billy yells, "You're a bully! You're hurting my girl!"
Sam punches Billy's belly and makes Billy hurl.

Joy pulls her pal, Billy, back up to his feet.

Wipes dirt off his face and makes his shirt neat.

Billy tells Joy strongly, "I've got to be a man

And put the finishing touches on my 'get-back-at-him' plan."

Billy tells Joy, "We will get him tonight.
During the campout, when he's tucked in so tight,
We will sneak in his tent while he's huddled in bed.
You bring the clippers and we'll both shave his head."

They put paint on their faces and dressed in pitch black,
Then snuck out of their tent through a thin, tiny crack.
They went down to Sam's tent in the midst of the night
To once and for all, put an end to this fight.

This is Billy's chance and he's not going to lose.

They laugh at poor Sam while he's taking a snooze.

Billy has the clippers and is ready to cut,

Then he gets this bad feeling deep down in his gut.

Joy stops all of a sudden and
has a question for Billy.
She asks, "Please don't get mad,
though this may sound quite silly.
Do you really think we should give him a trim?
Doesn't that make us as evil as him?"

Just then, Sam awoke and heard what was said.
He turns on the light and jumps out of his bed.
Sam's jaw drops wide open with nothing to say.
He is thankful his hair is still here to stay.

A little tear forms and drops from Sam's eye.

He hugs Billy and Joy; they all start to cry.

"I am sorry," he says. "I will not be mean again!"

Billy and Joy forgive him and forever, they're friends.

About the Author:

Kenneth L. Doane II was born and raised in Worcester County, Massachusetts. He is a former professional wrestler who has spent his career traveling around the world inspiring both children and adults to pursue their dreams. In addition to being the author of this book, Kenneth is also a dedicated student at Nichols College in Dudley, Massachusetts, pursuing a Bachelor's Degree in Sports Management. He has been featured in several newspapers, books, and television shows spotlighting his career and charitable contributions. When Kenneth is not wrestling, writing, or learning, he enjoys spending quality time with his family in Massachusetts and New York and visiting schools and organizations as a motivational speaker. Kenneth continues to raise awareness for this platform. His goal is to engage, educate, and inspire others to join the movement and prevent bullying all over the world. You too can join the ANTI-Bully Revolution at facebook.com/billysbully.

About the Illustrator:

Jason Boucher is a talented artist who calls the town of Southbridge, Massachusetts, his home. A graduate of Bay Path Regional Vocational Technical High School, Boucher is essentially self-taught having no formal secondary art training and yet specializes in all mediums including oils, acrylics, water colors, colored pencil, pastels, airbrushing, sculpting, and carvings. The thirty-five year old is owner of Jay Boucher Studios in Southbridge. His dream in life is to have a piece of his work exhibited in a museum somewhere and to be recognized as being a good husband, a good father, and a good artist. Boucher is engaged to be married to Erika Carlson in the fall of 2013 and has two sons, Beau and Blake, and step daughter, Kayla. Boucher's life mantra is based on a quote by former PGA golfer Ken Venturi who said, "I don't believe you have to be better than everybody else. I believe you have to be better than you ever thought you could be."